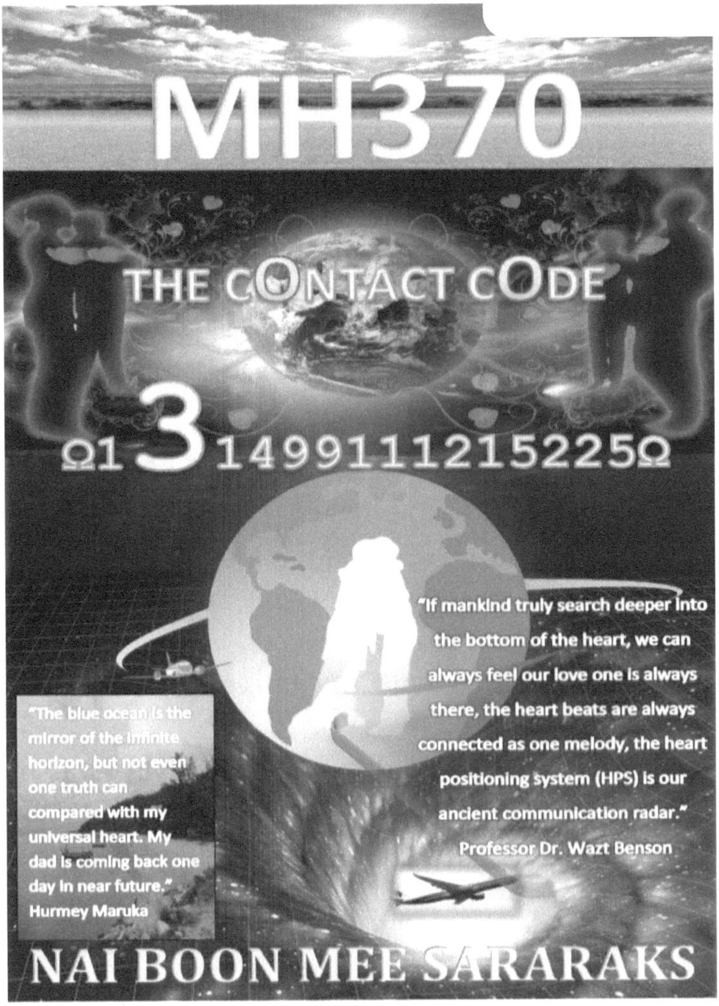

Copyright by Nai Boon Mee Sararaks (2017)

CHAPTER 1

"The blue ocean is the mirror of an infinite horizon, but not even one truth can compared with my universal heart. My dad is coming back one day." Hurmey Maruka smile and looking up into the wide blue sky near the sea in the nearby city she live in. Birds flew pass the horizon, plane flew from one route to another.

An earth is an amazing place for human living during the past and future but not today. Day by day everyone has their own story to tell. Story

Copyright by Nai Boon Mee Sararaks (2017)

of life, story of financial planning, story of family planning, story of business minded people, story of kids, story of aviation, story of different economic industries, story in the cinemas, story of unconditional love, just for sharing with others and many more stories people to peoples shared all over the world. Why did peoples share their stories?

Today am going to share with you a story, the hidden sight of flight MH370 went missing since 08 March year 2014, earth timeline. Families out there, in deep missed their missing loved one, but from year to years there is no solid evidenced and answered from the authority and independent researcher hardly given a solid proof to the public regarding the missing flight. How can this possible

Copyright by Nai Boon Mee Sararaks (2017)

while we are living in the modern earth, with a highly technology that mankind can flew to moon , mars planet discovery, and came back to earth planet? This is a story about a little girl appear in my dream and she was given a name by his late missing father; John Kepler Maruka, her name is Hurmey Maruka. One of the lonely girl living with her mother in a far advance city of love, in a country of the rising wisdom. This story is all about the creation of me, an author. I knew my words are not so well written, but I love to pen down part of my heart to all missing passengers, and families out there which is I am concern from the bottom of my heart.

Copyright by Nai Boon Mee Sararaks (2017)

"Mom, is been so long I've never seen my dad. I don't even have any visual of my dad. Mom, do you know where dad is right now?" Hurmey Maruka was at his landed house yard, enjoying her time star gazing every night. Her intention was inviting her dad to come back to earth planet.

"Can you please stop it! Don't mention it again, is been years so long, answer never return back to our family. Why asking where ? Where? and where dad is right now? How can mom answer your silly question while the authority can't?"

"Mom, …

Breath in…

Copyright by Nai Boon Mee Sararaks (2017)

…calm down mom. Why kept yourself stressed in this matter? He is your husband right? and he is my dad too, I have my right to asked."

"Do you think… do you think mum can give you an answer?" Stacy Celia Hurmey recall his memories of her past while she with her late missing husband. Her eyes blink with lovely tears, tears of memories, and tears of love through time unexpectedly she cannot control herself in front of her lovely daughter.

"Mom, I love you mom." Hug immediately. Hurmey Maruka slowly wiped out her mom tears with her little fingers. Her name was a combination of love by her mom and dad falling apart in a unknown distance. A distance which

Copyright by Nai Boon Mee Sararaks (2017)

totally a mystery of the aviation history. Somehow, as a little girl of herself; she knew that her mom could not let go her beloved husband forever and ever in life on earth. This is the time where her mum does not have time, each day is a waiting queue journey. At the age of eleven years old, she always had a dream to become a Astronomer. She is now in her journey to further her university journey in a nearby city of love. She believe that her dad is still some where alive. She believe in her own love, her own strength of liberty, and the thoughts that flew through her, she knew something must be done somewhere in her life sooner in the future. As she grew up with a success education result, her mom was so happy and proud

Copyright by Nai Boon Mee Sararaks (2017)

that her only daughter in the family was a smart girl followed her father.

In her life, few journeys of moments which her friends has but for her is an empty moment. With only a three letter words, and six letter words separate her life with the reality world she stayed. Although she had a great result in high school examination that qualify her to enroll in her university soon, for her part of the earth is in a distance of silent. Listening to her inner love apart of her name was her missing beloved father.

"Mom, can we celebrate dad birthday this year. Is been for a very long time mom not celebrate dad's birthday anymore. I mean, can I

Copyright by Nai Boon Mee Sararaks (2017)

buy a cake for dad this year before enroll in university?"

"Errr… I knew you my little girl. Sure, but one thing to tell you dear, is not mom do not want to celebrate birthday with dad; the frequent I celebrate yearly, the more I will think of him every night. Do you know it was a day to days and year to years nightmare mom ever had in life?".

"I understood mom. But don't you think the deeper we think of dad is the answer to contact him?"

"You mean?"

"I mean, we can know where is dad if we know how to contact him, a way, steps, or some

Copyright by Nai Boon Mee Sararaks (2017)

formula that can make a contact of humanity wirelessly".

"How silly you my little girl, you're going to university in couple of months, don't be silly thinking of silly idea like this."

"Mom, this is not silly. It is an idea. A thinking from myself every time I think of dad. Every time I look up into the night stars, I think of dad same as mom too. But, in the deeper thought I have a little mind burning inside my head, asking me to let mom knows that dad is still alive somewhere in this universe, somewhere on the earth layers, somewhere some time in some unknown place."

Copyright by Nai Boon Mee Sararaks (2017)

"Hurmey Hurmey,… Maruka Maruka… that goes your name again and again. Can't you be bored think of all this silly thing? Ok, mom believe in you but don't go further. The further you go, you might get lost. I do not want to lose you too. You're my precious moments, you're my precious love of all in this little family. Remember, don't forget to call mom when you are at the University soon. Life over there are very challenging and wonderful before you enter working life."

"Sure mom, I will. But, mom don't you ever think that dad can come back one day?"

"How possible you guess?"

"Mom, very possible. As easy as remove two letter words of impossible. 'I' and 'M', this

Copyright by Nai Boon Mee Sararaks (2017)

two words can be the cure of mom and the others families out there whom are now still missed their love one. We are all in the same mind, and the same circle of waiting the unexpected journey of life."

"Can you? If you can proof to mom how you can 'I' and 'M' become a reality, then you would save the entire families out there."

"Yeah! Wonderful mom, not all the time mom came to support my concern here in the same matter of moms' mind."

"Of course, let me tell you one secret that I think is time for mom to let you know."

Copyright by Nai Boon Mee Sararaks (2017)

"What secret is that mom? Let me know, let me know…"

"Wait, let mom get inside and take some refreshment juice for you and mom and mom will tell you slow and sweet."

"What juice mom want? Let me get it for you, you just remain seated here. Let me do it."

"No, no, let me do. You sit here."

"No, no. Let me mom."

"Ok, ok. Little girl argue to be the little house waitress."

"Let be me, the waitress. Is my pleasure. Mom, you remain seated here and think carefully

Copyright by Nai Boon Mee Sararaks (2017)

what you want to talk to me, about moms' secret. Anyway what juice do mom want to drink?"

"Give me a mixture of lemon, apple, and half of avocado blend. No ice please."

"Mom! You sure this is your drink? You never drink this weird drink before, how can this be yours today?"

"Just do it! Just do it! Listen to me, and I'll let you know the secret after you've done. Oh ya, just make yourself any juice you love at our lovely fruits kitchen. I'll wait you here. Hurry!"

"Ok mom, I'll be right back very soon."

Hurmey Maruka went inside her self renovated fruits kitchen by his missing father

Copyright by Nai Boon Mee Sararaks (2017)

leaved over. She did not know that this kitchen was build by her father. She walk inside the kitchen, at the right of the kitchen, there is a spiral arrangement of apple and at the left there is a spiral arrangement of orange. Both spiral was an entrance of the kitchen, a welcome spiral to the fruits kitchen .

A place where her mom called the kitchen, the heaven kitchen by my beloved husband. It was a small compartment that her husband did by himself 3 months before he on board. A kitchen filled of fruits, although in a family of two, fruits is not the reason to be empty at the kitchen. The space of the fruits heaven kitchen always filled with different types of fruits. The most important

Copyright by Nai Boon Mee Sararaks (2017)

section was the two spiral of fruits must be filled all time. The orange and apple, welcoming the family to the fruits kitchen. Next, lemon hexagon arrangement must be filled at the center of the fruits kitchen. How to know the center of the fruits kitchen? The center of the fruits kitchen was counted the combination foot steps of John Kepler Maruka, and Stacey Maruka. Each of them measure the kitchen with steps. To the left, 7 steps of Stacey and to from the right, 11 steps of her beloved husband. The center is the remaining one step in the center featured a design of hexagon shaped to be filled the yellow lemon for cooking, juice, and kitchen use. This is the unique of her husband, and the brilliant of Hurmey Maruka father. How could one individual build a self

Copyright by Nai Boon Mee Sararaks (2017)

design fruits kitchen just by using the combination of husband and wife. In that time, Hurmey Maruka yet born to earth. It was a sweet loving time where husband and wife are together. Both playing fruits together, cutting fruits and making fruits juice together. It was also a time where a loving couple like them do not have any thoughts in mind about the outer world, and the world where now separated apart from home, family and an unknown distance of reality and mystery. Here, here and here was the center of their entire landed house, the center of the lovely house. They named it as 'My lemon, my home, my husband my wife' a place where both unite as one and build an environment of wonderful colors creation by fruits.

Her beloved father said,

Copyright by Nai Boon Mee Sararaks (2017)

"This is the eleven steps of our home paradise." Until now, her wife still do not understand deeper what is the meaning of the eleven steps of our home paradise. What she know is the mixed of seven steps and eleven steps of husband and wife, deeper inside was nothing much more important than just a fruits kitchen.

Blender sound gather with the birds over the window arrived just next to the fruits kitchen.

"Hey you! I want some fruits to eat!" Birds calling from out side.

"Go way! Birds don't eat fruits".

"I want fruits, I want one strawberry!" Jumping outside the open window.

Copyright by Nai Boon Mee Sararaks (2017)

"Okie, okie, you want my favorite juice fruits? I can only give you one fruit. Here you go!", talking herself in the fruits kitchen and give one of the strawberry to the bird out side, just next to the window.

The bird are brave enough not to fly away, the bird just stand still and wait for the only strawberry. The bird ate the strawberry happily. Without flying, while eating while seeing inside the kitchen.

"Daring bird you! Aren't you going to fly with the strawberry?"

"Am not going to fly, am eating now. This is the place I birth. I birth here right up there just the

Copyright by Nai Boon Mee Sararaks (2017)

next green little tree of your yard." A language where mankind do not understand at all.

Hurmey Maruka continue making fruits juice. While she was making her fruits juice, she has a little thoughts in mind.

"Where did this bird came from? A very dare bird waiting to be a little companion of my strawberry juice."

Juice are in the making, It was a hot sunny day in the afternoon. Her mum prefer fresh without ice, and for herself she prefer the cold blended strawberry juice.

Bird be the companion of mankind on earth. A best buddy to entertain is to sing like a bird. In

Copyright by Nai Boon Mee Sararaks (2017)

the singing moment, brave is the answer of all food. If one bird do not have the braveness, how can a bird get employed and receive income and buy just only one strawberry? It was a day that Hurmey Maruka waiting for, the day to unlock the moms' secret. She do not know what her mom about to say, she do not know what is all about in her mom mind. What she know is the weird drink that her mom not even drink in her lifetime, the juice of the three weird fruits; the apple, the lemon and the avocado. In the world of the busy day out there, leave the two of this family making fruits juice, and a secret by mom. There would be so many stories happening now from so many families out there, is not the matter of a simple making fruits juice story and a secret. Wonder, what is the secret?

Copyright by Nai Boon Mee Sararaks (2017)

CHAPTER 2

"**SECRET**, mom, is time for

secret! Here you go your apple, lemon and avocado mixed juice. Maybe is your weird juice, mom. How can someone out there on earth planet can drink this juice. Avocado, Lemon, and Apple." Hurmey Maruka with apron and serve her lovely mom.

"Thank you Ms. Waitress. So kind and sweet of you preparing this wonderful weird juice."

"Is my pleasure, my mom."

Copyright by Nai Boon Mee Sararaks (2017)

"Take a sit now, oh! Little girl, can you take off your apron. Do you want me to tell you the 'secret'… hand sign show to her daughter.

…with the appearance like a real fruits juice waitress? Take off, take off. I can't continue with this look."

"Ok, ok mom. I take off now." Immediately she took off and put at one corner of the chair.

Both of the are sitting at the outside of their landed house, watching the garden view. Flowers planted by her mother, roses, sun flower, and a small lotus pond with the shape of love. The lotus pond in love shape was build by her beloved father. It was a great legend leave over from kitchen to the

Copyright by Nai Boon Mee Sararaks (2017)

yard in front. What else can be the leave over legend of an unique father?

"The wind today are so touchy, can you feel it?"

"Yeah, just feel good with the juice am drinking now. Mom, why don't you drink the juice I made? Ahhh! Mom not brave to drink?"

"No, it is not the matter of brave. It is the matter of time, a mind over matters that see through me and you ever since you're yet born on earth."

You mean? This juice relates to me too?

Yeah, it relates to you. This was your dad favorites juice.

Copyright by Nai Boon Mee Sararaks (2017)

Really? Oh my! I never think of this before. Does the taste good?

"Not really, it was my first time drink this. Since your dad leave, and since your dad around here with me. I've never drink his self juice creation.

"Wonderful! More , more , is this the secret?"

Yes, this is just the beginning of my secret.

"Beginning?, continue mom. Lovely to listen now."

"This is just the beginning…" mom remain silent then, flowing inside her mind in a sudden

Copyright by Nai Boon Mee Sararaks (2017)

space and time. Pause the conversation with her daughter.

"Mom, Mom! Can you hear me, hello…"

"Yes, yes, I can listen to you. Am here."

"What happen to you mom, why suddenly our secret in a sudden pause?"

"…the beginning of your journey before you were birth. three months before your dad on board on the flight, he change his favorite juice recipe in adding an avocado in to the both lemon and apple. An add value to this drinks take me a lot of curiosity in my mind what is actually your dad trying to taste, and what is all about the juice can be the answer of a synchronicity of your existence

Copyright by Nai Boon Mee Sararaks (2017)

now. His actual favorite juice was apple and lemon. Takes him as the favorites juice since the first day I met him in a fruits juice bar in a little corner of the city here. The fruits owner is still running the business now, probably took over by his son now."

"What is all about with adding avocado?"

"Am not sure, my dear. What I knew from your dad is he did told me that adding an avocado is an add value of having you to this world. With just apple and lemon are not enough for both of us. He also said, avocado is the relation of the secret of my future baby. That time, you're almost close to six months of my pregnancy. 3 months later, he was announced by the government missing on board for his architecture business venture. Your

Copyright by Nai Boon Mee Sararaks (2017)

dad was a very amazing designer, and architecture. You see here, the pond, the yard, even the flowers are planted by him. As you can see our fruits kitchen, was a legacy leave over by your dad. This was a repeated story telling for you my dear little girl since you were in my tummy."

"Did you asked dad further about the avocado, and what it means by the future of his baby, which mean me today?"

"Yes, mom did asked him more on this matter. What does Avocado real mean to you. He said, in a future years everything in this world will be change, even mankind itself one day all of them will change totally. From someone become no one, and from no one become someone, further more

Copyright by Nai Boon Mee Sararaks (2017)

from one become zero, and zero be the hero. That time I was totally blurred of his talk. He said with only faith and trust, one can only move forward with change and also with also faith and trust one can destroy almost everything in this world included the creation itself. Like the juice, apple and lemon taste is just good. If avocado is added, what would it be next? Can it be the same taste of the juice remain or become worst or become a hidden clue of an unknown juice recipe for my wife to drink?"

"So, it means Avacado is the hidden clue of an unknown juice recipe, have mom drink it?"

Nope, this is why mom asked you to make for me. You about to leave this lovely house for

Copyright by Nai Boon Mee Sararaks (2017)

your education journey soon, is my honor to tell you this. Dad do told me, don't ever give to our son or daughter to drink while am here with you. He said, only drink when one day am not with you anymore. That time, that moment I felt a little sad, because in sudden he said about he is to leave my entire life for a sudden. Moreover, mom gave it a joke for your dad.

"Oh mom, don't tell me you going to ask me to drink this? No, No!"

"Yes, you must drink this. Remember, this is the only secret that your dad told me not to let you drink."

Copyright by Nai Boon Mee Sararaks (2017)

"No, mom first, Mom first. You the one asked me to make for you this drink. I will drink after mom. Deal?"

"Ok, deal!"

The drink was so greenish in color. A little brown as red apple was the chosen one and it was all the while in the fruits kitchen fully filled with red color apples. That was my father favorites fruits. Somehow, if am going to drink this It would be a raw sour lemon taste, and sweetest red apply taste in a juicy blend without ice. Oh my! Added with avocado, would smell buttery, and a little bitter? Salty? Sweet? What the world am living now, as I yet taste any avocado on earth.

"Hello! What are you thinking at?"

Copyright by Nai Boon Mee Sararaks (2017)

No, no mom. I was thinking of the taste of this juice. Would it taste good mom? Mom first to taste ya. Ha..ha..!

"Ermm..maybe taste good, maybe a new great taste for both of us. It would be a new coming taste of our family, then you can make it yourself when you're in the University education stay later on."

"Mom, have you tried avocado before? I yet to taste it though."

"Slightly tasted buttery, you know like a butter on a loaf of bread? You know like a fresh cream? You know like a peanut butter? You know like a cheese cream?"

Copyright by Nai Boon Mee Sararaks (2017)

"Ya, ya. Eeeeaaaaaauuuuuuuuu! What a taste on earth!"

Taking their sweet time exploring the taste of the three choice of juice, wondering if you would be one of them in this journey asking dads' favorites juice? and the few months back before missing flight MH370, did any words of curiosity start to pop out from the soul of love.

Mankind are very soft in the sense of observation all over knowledge guide by teacher and even own husband and wife. Like the juice that matters mom and daughter. It was a day when everyone share the same question what is happening to our beloved one. What is actually happened to our world today from the past, now

Copyright by Nai Boon Mee Sararaks (2017)

and coming future. Is been years after the missing, years…

A long moment in each and everyone of us had go through the time on earth, day by day kept thinking of the important conversation with our loved one before he or she flew on board. A conversation like an avocado for my baby. As just a little taste of avocado conversation can carry the seed of the future, would it be a great journey for a big change to our earth? Peoples mind today might not think as deeper as it goes, but for Hurmey Maruka it would be the other way round of what's people thinking now she is totally different. She can imagine that one day she can able to contact with her lost missing dad. She believe that the

Copyright by Nai Boon Mee Sararaks (2017)

flight MH370 was still somewhere in the air. She knew it was there and one day she will able to contact her father.

Hurmey Maruka was a brave girl, a girl followed her father steps, be creative in all thoughts she creates. She would be a possible journey that will make you feel how can our mind can totally be and set into a center point of our mind like how we people on earth fine-tuning our radio signal while waiting for the perfect wave and listen to the melody arrived through into the tunnel of our pair of ears.

Hurmey Maruka believe that everyone in this world has their own guidance, the guidance of the perfect mind; our brightest side of our self is

Copyright by Nai Boon Mee Sararaks (2017)

the true pathway and always present for all matters happened. It is just the matter of time which we need to slowly tune in, search for the perfect wave and we will understand the journey of our perfect mind.

While bird and birds around them are singing together, birds do not know what is the story behind the house owner. What these birds knew is hunting for food, survive, time to go back home, and fruits kitchen asking for strawberry. Maybe these birds knew that in this lovely family house, missing one person which is the missing father.

Take a breath in, and breath out.

Copyright by Nai Boon Mee Sararaks (2017)

"Mom! Am taking my breath in now before my turn to drink this 'awesome' fruits juice by our lovely dad. Don't you need a to get some fresh breath in before taste it for the first ever in mom life?"

"Ya, good idea my dear lovely daughter."

Breath in by her mom. Again and again. Slowly move forward to her lips. A transparent jug of her husband fruits juice recipe. Close to her lips, very close and very very close to her lips. The juice crawl over to her mouth, lips, and teeth.

"Eee…mmmmmm…cccccccc…"

Taste good? How's the taste mom, pretty good? Sweet?

Copyright by Nai Boon Mee Sararaks (2017)

"Not bad!", a pretty weird laugh in the loudly itchy sound by her mom, and hand over the juice mug to Hurmey Maruka.

Oh my goodness moment!

"Is yours now, is time for you to taste is. Finish it! is your dad asking me to lead you drink his special juice recipe. Just for you my dear."

"Again, my second goodness moment in my life. Ok, ok I will drink it all, hopefully with this moment I have, I can know more about my dad, and if possible I want to know where is my dad now."

Copyright by Nai Boon Mee Sararaks (2017)

"Is your pleasure of today and coming days, my little dear. I real hope your dad know that you're drinking his secret juice now."

Hurmey Maruka closed her nose. Breath in deeply, and the first part of the juice. Again she breath in.

"Oh! What the taste in the world I drink now mom? This is dad choice for me?"

"Ya, ya. Is all yours, finish it and I will wash the mug for you later."

"The taste smell like am drinking a mug of melted butter just under the hot sunny sun."

Her mom laugh. Her eyes focusing at the end of the city tallest building. Her eyes dripped a

Copyright by Nai Boon Mee Sararaks (2017)

little tears. One seconds, two seconds, three seconds. She washed away with her fingers thumb.

"You can share with your friends if you want. Anyway, mom do not know what is the internal good and benefits in drinking these mixed juice. You know?"

"No, I know nothing mom. Let me finish this first then we talk further ya."

Hurmey Maruka, breath in again. She slowly and lovely finished the second half of the juice in the mug. One and for all, she proudly knew that her own father leave her a legacy of unknown mixed fruits juice which she will search more on the meaning given by her dad.

Copyright by Nai Boon Mee Sararaks (2017)

"Yeah! Finished. Mom, I make it to the final. The taste not that bad, just a little buttery, and oil from the avocado. Part of the juice, is also a feel of drinking olive oil."

"Really? Sound pretty good for you. How do you feel further, will you taste it again?"

"No, no. Maybe next time. Now today again!"

Remember, this was the only drink your dad hand over me to hand over to you incase he is not around anymore.

Mom, he is still somewhere out there. Believe me mom! Dad is still alive. I feel it mom. Don't mention it again, not around anymore ok!

Copyright by Nai Boon Mee Sararaks (2017)

Ok, will never said again.

Promise me mom?

Ok, I will promise you my dear little daughter.

Oh ya, nearly forget. How far from our home here the fruits shop dad and mom met up the first time?

Not that far, just the next junction of the busy city. A lovely shop at the right of the junction, if mom not mistaken it is just beside the old books shop.

"Thanks mum."

"Why? You want to meet the owners' handsome boy which is now running the fruits

Copyright by Nai Boon Mee Sararaks (2017)

business? Ha! Caught you now, have a heart to meet him, am sure you well feel on your first thoughts."

"No, no. Am not suppose to be in mom mind now. I knew what mom going to said to me. All about love in the first sight, am I right? Is this you both met the first?" smiling face pointed to her mom.

"Ya, It was still fresh in my mind. Mom still remember the first item that your dad choose the same as mine. Our both hand met in the same one item."

"What item is that mom, mind to let me know? Come on Mom, tell me?"

Copyright by Nai Boon Mee Sararaks (2017)

"It's the Yellow Lemon which now position at the center of our fruits kitchen."

"Wow, both of you are so romantic. It can be one of the visual where always screen in the movie, mom!"

"Yellow lemon, sound filled with energy on your first touch, mom."

"Energy?"

"Ya, energy. Lemon is energy."

How can your mind tune in that word. Just the same like your dad. He did told me, again and again that our love is like an energy. Both of us love and all over the world couples, and married couples are all energy. Although is sour, but we

Copyright by Nai Boon Mee Sararaks (2017)

must brave enough to understand the sweetest moment when we add a little sugar in and make some lemonade juice. Your dad favorites sugar, brown sugar.

"Wonderful mom, I think am going to the fruits grocer this coming weekend. I am going to ask the shop perfect person about avocado and further dig into what's dad actually want me to know about this avocado."

"Come on, it is just a drink. Not more than that."

"No, no, mom. If dad can say for the future baby, is me and am pretty sure there must be something synchronized me with avocado and my missing dad. Am going to search more on this, and

Copyright by Nai Boon Mee Sararaks (2017)

one day on earth I will be able to contact dad for the first time in my life, I will and I will contact with dad. Although I did not see my dad face since am born, listen to his voice through my ears since am born; mom, believe me! Am going to proof what dad said is something much more value than just a little avocado and secret juice of three mixture of fruits."

The burning spirit of Hurmey Maruka begin to look forward in her life as her life turning point, a journey where she start to explore in bringing back the hope of her father to return home.

Everyone in this world are putting in hope year by years for the return of the missing passengers in a safe journey back home. Although

Copyright by Nai Boon Mee Sararaks (2017)

the timeline is years back, I believe something might be wrong somewhere in this earth planet. Either humanity exploring the other side of our greatest technology and economic standard, or our earth sea is too deep that unable to trace any floating debris anywhere around the world on the sea, nothing floating is concern to be relates with the missing flight MH370.

Hope and pray is the only answer for peoples out there while waiting for authorities to search and release any latest news in the media. But, for Hurmey Maruka it is more than a search, hope and pray.

She is exploring the deeper side of her dads' avocado message trying to tell her that the missing

Copyright by Nai Boon Mee Sararaks (2017)

flight is related to the avocado, apple, and lemon. She is trying to understand the position stand by her dad, and the shoes put on her mom.

Also, she is concern the understanding of perfect mind thinking by the families out there whom the same concerned about their missing loved one.

Would a small avocado be the true message of her early pathway in getting more information about her dad? Or did she over heated her mind over matters of her beloved dad?

It would be a great huge impact for someone whom never ever see her own dad since birth, in a sudden was given a secret juice that possibility contain the knowledge of contacting her own dad

Copyright by Nai Boon Mee Sararaks (2017)

through a little deeper search on what's her mom

had given her, and is already moms' job to pass

down this long hidden moment with her husband

years, years, years… ago.

Copyright by Nai Boon Mee Sararaks (2017)

Chapter 3

LOVE, this is the city of love I

birth on the landed house. Since I was born in the time where everything in the past seen by my mom totally changed, it was no longer a city of time where beggars asked for money, cats at the road side hunting for food at the nearby rubbish bin, strangers seeing you like they are robbery's on call, few pictures of memories kept by my mom in her self home office little corner photos library.

My mom was a photo journalist, she published her own self taken photos in her own

Copyright by Nai Boon Mee Sararaks (2017)

online portal. My mum has her own business, managing a huge group of photographers around the world. My mom self home office designed by my dad again. I can say that I have a lovely wonderful dad leave behind so many moments to my mom and me my self with my lovely room enable me to open up the roof, and stargazing the stars move around the time while am falling asleep. It was so cool when you can tell your friends that your bed was a place that can also view stars at the same time, and sleep when it's about time to close our eyes.

Their time, my mom and dad time was a time where the earth is abandoned by the love, mostly half of the apple that I could eat, the

Copyright by Nai Boon Mee Sararaks (2017)

another half I need to put at the rubbish bin, because the other half is the rotten side of the apple.

Just imagine, if I were born in that time; I could surely bring half of what I have now to peoples over there. Sadly, this is not my time. My mom said, this is not the only sole city of love. There are much more other countries, places, and some places in the landed hills, and landed mountains got the same status of what I experience now.

All are cities around the world are in the similar practiced, the peoples walk past you would just open their mouth and greets you good morning, happy day, good day, hello, have a wonderful day brother, have a awesome moments sister, and most

Copyright by Nai Boon Mee Sararaks (2017)

of the languages spokes over here, they kept repeated the same at the end of greetings, with brothers and sisters. I felt just a normal wish and a well practice time over here wishing peoples all over around while am walking down the street. Peoples here are so amazing, their mouths would just non stop greetings which ever people they make eyes contact with.

My mom said, this was not in her time maybe the entire humanity during her time are yet ready for all this goodness act. Eventually, I am now walking down in the busy street searching for the fruits shop where my mom and dad make their first contact.

Copyright by Nai Boon Mee Sararaks (2017)

How can a lovely couple in the beginning filled with love and an energy, separated in the distance of unknown mystery since the year 2014. I just imagine, if I was in my mom shoes; I probably never to forget the sweetest time where the first contact in each and everyone relationship moments on earth.

In my own quote, when we start to discover the further side of the universe, the universe will automatically responded to our distance of mind. How far can we peoples on earth explore the beauty of all stars? It was an amazing journey discover the names of stars while I am on bed thinking of my beloved father. One over so many stars, I always attracted to the star with the name,

Copyright by Nai Boon Mee Sararaks (2017)

Mintaka. A star that line up along the Orion belt, Mintaka (Delta Orionis, 34 Ori) is 915 light years away and shines with magnitude 2.21. Mintaka is 90,000 times more luminous than the Sun. Mintaka is a double star. The two stars orbit around each other every 5.73 days. This was one of my favorite star gazing all night before sleeping.

Am walking down the street, I saw strangers cats eating at the corner of the city. Food are well prepared for them.

I saw strangers dog, another corner of the city eating their food well prepared by the peoples for them.

My mom did said, in her time dogs and cats leave over in the city hunting for food all over the

Copyright by Nai Boon Mee Sararaks (2017)

place like beggars values their time for minimum cost of living.

I walk and walk, but cannot find the fruits shop in the city told by my mum. A girl walk past in front me, I will try to ask her then.

"Good day sister!"

"Good day to you too, sister. How can I help you?", replied the girl she approached.

"Do you know any fruits store nearby the city here?"

"You mean Fruits Rainbow grocer?"

"Hmm...I don't know the name, but my mom told me it's just close to an old books store. Correct me if am wrong?"

Copyright by Nai Boon Mee Sararaks (2017)

"Yes, it is just close to the old books store. Just the end of this pedestrian, and turn right you will find your fruits shop then."

"Thank you, sister."

"You're most welcome. Have a good day."

"Yes, you too. Good day."

Copyright by Nai Boon Mee Sararaks (2017)

CHAPTER 4

FRUITS RAINBOW,

the brand was glowing up in the busy city of love. While peoples are busy walking up and down in the busy street, fruits lovers stopped by and purchase their fruits. Some peoples busy in their journey to workplace, they purchased cut fruits and refresh their body.

I saw many peoples in the fruits grocer, while am waiting for the perfect time for the perfect guy that am waiting for, I would just find a place just opposite the fruits grocer for my morning coffee and catching up his time when no

Copyright by Nai Boon Mee Sararaks (2017)

one walk in the fruits grocer, that is the best I can ask many question about my dad mystery juice.

Coffee is one of the morning 'must' drink routine for Hurmey Maruka. Without a single dips of coffee on her tongue, she would feel uneasy, and sometime she will fall asleep. Night before sleep, and evening for tea time; best practice for her is drinking her favorites strawberry juice.

She wait for the time, about 30 minutes over. Finally the fruits shop opposite was just the boy and two other workers. She's about time for her first explore in her life.

"Excuse me, pay the bill please." A waiter then bring the coffee bill to her.

Copyright by Nai Boon Mee Sararaks (2017)

"Excuse me, sister. Here is the bill. $3.70 in a total."

"Here you go, keep the balance as your tips. Thank you for your great service."

"You're welcome."

Hurmey Maruka walk off the coffee shop and walk across the road.

The balance of $0.40 then was placed in the coin box. The coin box wrapped with a pink color art design with the name, helping the poor dogs and cats out there.

This is the culture of the city of love in the time she was raised up. Somehow, missing her own dad is the only way for her to be different in

Copyright by Nai Boon Mee Sararaks (2017)

the search for the truth what is actually happening

to her dad for the past, years after years on

searching with no solid documentation of proof. If

you seat in the corner of the shop and could smell

the coffee from the barista maker, it was the smell

of the coffee, the aroma flew through the air

hugging on the particles of coffee smell in the

atom and arrived for your warm welcoming coffee

drink, and you knew it that your drinks is about to

serve. But for this missing flight MH370, even

smell and debris are confusing the public even all

families. Can the earth be so small? Or the earth is

too big for humanity to live on over the time,

centuries, and day after days? How possible a girl

like her has the passion and hope in making what

she think a battle in her mind, thinking her father

Copyright by Nai Boon Mee Sararaks (2017)

all day looking up to the stars while she sleep, and fought for her mom love adore.

"Welcome to Fruits Rainbow!, have a great Saturday." Greeting and smiling over his face by Robert, a name tag pinned on his pink apron. I can see it. Was he the one am looking for?

"How can I assist you? We have plenty of fruits today. Most of the fruits just arrive. Any fruits you need, I be your assistant." Robert smile to Hurmey, and welcoming her with proud on his eyes.

"Sure, thank you Mr.Robert."

"Oh, you knew my name?"

Copyright by Nai Boon Mee Sararaks (2017)

"Ya." Hurmey smile and pointed at his name tag.

"Thank you. It was lovely time dining into our store today." Robert adjusted his name tag pinned on his shirt.

Hurmey smile, her eyes focus into Robert eyes for few seconds and change her attention at the cashier counter. There is another guy pack some fruits.

"Is he the guy my mom said?, or this lovely Robert is the one. That guys was in the counter packing some fruits and I cannot see his full face, as he is with his cap on. Never mind, just forget it. I will ask this lovely charming guy in front of me then." Just a few seconds tripped in her mind,

Copyright by Nai Boon Mee Sararaks (2017)

Hurmey Maruka journey into the center of who is the real boy behind the owner of this shop, son.

Seeing all over the corner of the grocer looking for all fruits. Three steps walk forward, and Robert walk backward 3 steps.

Robert hand grappled something on his hand,

Hurmey Maruka then in the same time too grappled the same item. The touch of Hurmey palms landed on Robert fingers.

"Opps, am sorry. Robert leaf up his hand. Sorry, I did not mean that."

"Is ok, don't have to worry about that."

"Oh ya! This is the fruits of the day, Saturday the avocado day!"

Copyright by Nai Boon Mee Sararaks (2017)

"Really?"

"Yes, every Saturday was our avocado day. Is this the fruits you looking for?"

"Yes, yes. This is not vegetable?"

"No. Avocado is not vegetable, it is a fruits. You might be inclined as a vegetable because of its green hue and savory taste, but the avocado is technically a fruit."

"Really, how can it be a fruits when it's green?"

"Oh then, name me how can a green apple be a fruits when it is in green too?"

Copyright by Nai Boon Mee Sararaks (2017)

"Ok, go ahead. What is next, have you see the plant, is it huge or like other similar vegetables plants."

"More specifically, it is a single-seeded berry size, A fruit is "the matured ovary of a flower, and the plant is not so tall, you can even plug the fruits by your hand."

"Can we plant it at home?"

"Sure, you can too plant at your home with the condition of suitable weather."

"Wonderful! I have one question, is this avocado a mystery fruit among all fruits?"

"What did you mean mystery, hunted? Magic?"

Copyright by Nai Boon Mee Sararaks (2017)

"No, no, I mean..eeehmmm; Just forget it."

"Actually, if you want to know more. I can tell you that, avocado is the fruits of celebrities out there around the world."

"Celebrities fruits? You mean most of them out there ate avocado all days in their life?"

"Yes, yes they do. They ate avocado 4-5 days a week, especially during the time when our sun about to rise."

"How do they eat? Raw like this, cut and eat?"

"They eat with bread, union, salad, oranges slices and some they toasted with garlic, and a

Copyright by Nai Boon Mee Sararaks (2017)

little Himalaya salt on it. For them they did told me, taste good."

"Why did they eat this weird food?"

"For them, it's a fruit to sustain their hungriness. To reduce having lots of fat in their body, and good appetited for them skipping lunch. For them, it is a energetic fruits that kept them slim. Maybe, I never try before."

"Wow. It was so cool."

"Any other great information than this about avocado."

"Yes, it is also good in reducing our acidity level in our body health guide."

Copyright by Nai Boon Mee Sararaks (2017)

Hurmey excited to know more and more, before go deeper into the conversation. She ask in sudden.

"Is you the owner of this shops' son?" while asking, she look at the counter at the other end of the shop. Robert look over the counter too. Pretend no to disclose his identity.

"Is you?"

"Emm, yes… my dad leave over his shop to me. How do you knew about my dad?"

"Oh, my mom used to buy fruits here during her young time. Guess so, my mum knew you dad maybe."

Copyright by Nai Boon Mee Sararaks (2017)

"Oh, the world is so small. Having us today meeting up here, while your mom was our customers too."

"Yes, it was a place where my mum met my dad."

"What a lovely moment you parent have."

"Not anymore now…"

In sudden silent.

"Am sorry."

"…not anymore, but maybe soon near future."

"What did you mean? They both separated?"

"Ya, long time ago."

Copyright by Nai Boon Mee Sararaks (2017)

"Divorced?"

"No. Not really."

"Then? Sorry mind to ask further?"

"My dad was one of the passengers in the missing flight MH370."

"Sorry, am sorry to hear this. Come have a seat. Come, come, have a seat. I will bring you a juice make by my self just for you."

"No, no. Is ok."

"Don't worry, this is my treat for you. My pleasure, as a customer walk in. Come have a seat. Give me few minutes, I'll make a juice for you."

Copyright by Nai Boon Mee Sararaks (2017)

"Thanks, Robert. Don't you ask me what juice I want to drink before you make it?"

"Let me guess, Strawberries juice without milk?"

"How did you knew that was my favorites juice?"

"Oh, you eyes told me that was your favorites. Wait for me ok, take a look of our grocer upcoming promotion fruits booklet, while I go and make it for you. Stay calm, and don't worry much about your past, let's take the present as the beginning of the future."

"Ok, I'll take noted on into my life."

Copyright by Nai Boon Mee Sararaks (2017)

Robert went inside the juice bar, pick up the fresh arrival strawberries and wash with the water. He then blend fresh strawberry juice in just few seconds, insert ice cubes and a little ounce of water. He is ready to serve.

"Here you go, your favorites strawberry blended juice."

"Thank you. Lovely you."

"Welcome." Can I seat here with you, have some talking with you? First, I've yet to know your name after me, Robert."

"Yes, my name Hurmey. Hurmey Maruka. Nice to know you today. You can seat anyway, it's your owned shop."

Copyright by Nai Boon Mee Sararaks (2017)

"So, what makes you come here? To buy avocado fruits, I'll help you pack it?

"No, no…I still have a lot in my house."

"Really, avocado lovers too?"

"Not really, , is my dad. I will buy from you in my next visit when is about to finish."

"You dad still at home making juice or eating avocado?"

"No, not him. Is my mom. She distribute some juices to the nearby village peoples up at the hill whenever the villagers need juice they will just knock on my mom mobile."

"Don't the villagers up there make their own juice themselves?"

Copyright by Nai Boon Mee Sararaks (2017)

"No, my mom make for them and sustain our daily life with some exchange of vegetables, rice, and nuts, and some meals make by nearby neighbors."

"So, what makes your dad love avocado so much? He is also one of the celebrities, guess maybe?"

"No, he is a designer. An architecture for house and yard all over the world he had to travel all time."

"Guess, your dad need avocado for his daily routine then. Less eat, and boost up more energy and save time skipping lunch. Your dad body must be fit and slim.

Copyright by Nai Boon Mee Sararaks (2017)

"Yes, my dads' always remain healthy and slim. Mom always say he is slim guy in my memory inside my mind, I don't have any real live picture since I was born."

"Oh sorry to hear that. Do you have any latest news on the search?"

No. Not for now and always not for the past over years. But, one thing I have now is only avocado. Can avocado be the clue to find out my dad, would be possible for me to contact him through?

You mean avocado can help you search the missing flight?

Copyright by Nai Boon Mee Sararaks (2017)

"Yes, my dad leave me his legacy about avocado but I yet to know what's all about."

Hurmey Maruka told him about the weird juice leave by her dad from the beginning of the hair to head and to toe and dropped to the feet and ground of the land, Fruits Rainbow.

Robert was attracted to Hurmey life moments sharing. He also told Hurmey that life was not as easy as have a job, family and get a house, and have plenty of money for living. Life on earth is further more filters into different level of dimensional stage. A place where peoples live here on earth and create the lifestyle activities from day to day to sustain the living cost, and sustain the daily and monthly expenditure is just a mass.

Copyright by Nai Boon Mee Sararaks (2017)

Mass that you will never knew that time had burn over year to years knowing nothing we have ever done for the rest of our life, there is also a place where energy storage around the avocado seems to help celebrities kept slim and remain healthy lifestyle. The hidden energy is the place where we're all looking for. A place we call love. In each of every fruits has its different contain of energy level, lemon has it, apple has it and avocado has it too. When these three fruits unite as one juice, it boost up a different stage of energy for human being activity, to think, to keep life balance and some could just live long. Robert believe that these three fruits has its secret hidden energy that can boost the ability of mankind in connecting the inner love of our self, with another alike contacting

Copyright by Nai Boon Mee Sararaks (2017)

someone in the another land wirelessly. How can the world be so cruel to the good ones, and how can the good ones leave behind their loved one missing them all day. There must be some loops somewhere that need all of us to think deeper, and change the way we think in the past for the up coming brighter future using our self immune ability in knowing more how mankind on earth can live a longer life with fruits, how to connect our soul with fruits; utilized the different types of energy level contain in fruits. How to know more other hidden history of mankind which we had once live behind the fall of the old civilization once before. We are actuly far leave behind not because we are not well improve, but we are tense to followed what we've given all the time since the

Copyright by Nai Boon Mee Sararaks (2017)

day we're born. I my great grandfather time, they live without any cellphones, and internet, how can they communicate each other? There might be some ways where the history had once forget. There must be some other way that we ourselves yet discover. I believe nothing is impossible that what Hurmey said to me was a journey to the impossible moment where everyone unite into one thoughts in communicating with the missing one using love, through the secret juice leave over by her father.

I believe this is the perfect time to call all the passengers come back to earth, is time for them to stay happily ever after with the world leaders, and the world peoples in this time after years and

Copyright by Nai Boon Mee Sararaks (2017)

years after disasters rise in major some countries, almost half of civilization died frozen, died due to the burning hot sun, some place even worst covered up with sea levels.

The dry is wet, and the wet turns to dry place, and new diseases spread all over the world, they name it the 'mind syndrome' where most working and education peoples all over the world face the same syndrome. Some stayed in the hospitals for weeks, months, and years but cannot come back to live in a an unconscious stage, body could not move, but only eyes are aware of every seconds in fear state.

Doctors gave them a vaccine with the name '360ABN' the long form of ABN is 360

Copyright by Nai Boon Mee Sararaks (2017)

Authorized Batch Nine' that only cure to those are rich enough to pay, and is only given nine times in the first month, some rich peoples able to pay for, but chances are very slim enough for patient to recover.

For the poor families, they've to relay on time over matters of moments. Some families give up hope, without any waiting and cure through years, they pulled out the soul of the patient. Most peoples around the world do not know what is happening to the education wise people facing the same problem. For the early hood parents, they do not want their children to continue to high level studies, and remain their children work after high school. Cutting the journey of the soul while

Copyright by Nai Boon Mee Sararaks (2017)

waiting for cure is like killing the patient, someone's hope for long waiting.

So, am sure in this missing flight MH370, it was the same mind over matters that all families out there must remain this hope and never stop searching, discovering and wish upon time in near future that one day all families of missing passengers are able to communicate with their missing loved one through some ways which mankind yet discover.

Since years after years after years the missing flight 370 incident, the world had totally change drastically from the weather, to land, and to sea. Even the air route in some areas are restricted to flew through by planes to reach one destination,

Copyright by Nai Boon Mee Sararaks (2017)

one planes must use the long route, some even change the route every 3 to 6 days, according to the authorities, it was a practice to avoid some circumstances with other planes.

Somehow, after years again when the old turn silent, and the younger one stood up in taking care the humanity, finally we are free from all poor and pain. The patients from all over the world whom waited for so many years for the 'Mind Syndrome' finally cured with just a touch of one country leader.

Never knew after that, in sudden news spread all over the countries over this pain, so many new country leaders took over, all of them as young as early 20's, with a charming face, male

Copyright by Nai Boon Mee Sararaks (2017)

and female. This moment, nobody rise any matters that gender was the problem in ruling a country, but love does.

Countries leaders, in sudden heal all patient with just a touch where this country leaders appear from no where in sudden at the hospitals all over the world in taking over the case of the patients. To be the honest, most of the leaders was not in any high education level such as universities, college. Most of them just after high school.

It was the leader today, the city of love where we live here. It is also to believe that, this is the time where all of us are ready to bring back the flight MH370, for so long went missing and for so long there is no any updates by the authorities. For

Copyright by Nai Boon Mee Sararaks (2017)

Hurmey Maruka, I think this is just the beginning of the city of love, who knows Hurmey would be the next leaders of all leaders all over the world? The impossible journey is always start from '*I'm.*'

Almost one hour after conversation with this little girl, five years younger than me; I felt that she has a very bright future in discover new knowing about communicating someone from a distance using her own method she names to me. Everything started with the red apples, lemons, and avocado.

"That was interesting to hear from you Hurmey." Smile over his lips and eyes contact inner self to Hurmey.

Copyright by Nai Boon Mee Sararaks (2017)

"Thank you.", Hurmey replied with smile. Touching her heart with her right palms and smile with shine, her lips showing she is interested to talk more with this guy, Robert.

"I wish, I can help you in the search."

Don't worry about me, Robert. You need to take good care of this shop leave by your dad too. While you take good care of this shop, I will continue my search. Will keep you update."

"Sure. Thanks."

I've my time taken after you here, I got to move back to the hill before my mom ask me more later. Thank for your Strawberry juice drinks treat

Copyright by Nai Boon Mee Sararaks (2017)

for today. I will treat you next, coffee opposite your shop. Do you love coffee?"

"Yes, sure. I always had my breakfast over there."

"I will see you in my next visit here."

"Don't you want to buy some fruits?"

"Sure, pack me three red apples, seven yellow lemon and zero avocado. There's still leave a lot in my fruits storage."

"Sure, Let me pack it for you."

Hurmey then leave the Fruits Rainbow with smile, happily knowing something else are actually connect to her life. Robert smile too, waive hand back to Hurmey.

Copyright by Nai Boon Mee Sararaks (2017)

"Waiting for you good news! Bye."

Hurmey waive back hand to Robert. Walk down the street. Feeling confidence in knowing more about her explore begin here, in a fruits shop. She knew from today, everything in this world is connected to each other with reason why and with some hidden reason to know more. She turn her head looking back at the coffee shop, checking on her purchase bills from both coffee shop, and fruits grocer, she then smile and kept safely in her purse.

She look at her hand watch, the time is seven minutes past three in the evening.

Copyright by Nai Boon Mee Sararaks (2017)

CHAPTER 5

SCRYNONICITY is the string of all connection. This was told by Robert, the fruits grocer handsome son. I must remember this for now and forever. Be the person in discover the new pathway for mankind which once they had forgotten. How can we as human living on earth forget the sole of our ability to compare with today modern lifestyle where everything we need are given since the day we were born. Technology gadgets are used by kids, if they were not using this gadgets, they would cry loudly. This was not in the visual during my late grandfather time. My mom have picture of her grandpa when they were

Copyright by Nai Boon Mee Sararaks (2017)

still as little as kids. My grandpa holding few tree

brunch, and rocks with few self build muddy sand.

Now, you can see almost all kids today are playing

modern technology gadgets. How can we compare

our time today with theirs? The answer is there is

no limitation for limitation we use to see today. In

my case, I have no ways in finding a way to let

peoples out there in the same situation as mine to

know that the inner self of human being can be

connected to our earth magnetic field through the

thoughts create by our mind and vibrational touch

flow into our entire body. In getting this journey a

very close to my answer, am sure I must get

avocado, red apple and lemon as the gear up for

the connectivity begin. Like cars, you need petrol

to move, and if you fried something you need an

Copyright by Nai Boon Mee Sararaks (2017)

oil. If you need to success in life, you need to work smart and organized all our time accordingly and manage every single activity in our life usefully. Am having not much time after came back from Fruits Rainbow, letting my mom knows all about Robert, plan time for my first enrollment in the university. Lots I need to plan include my research on my dads' mystery juice. I knew it was a hard time getting all this done overnight. Somehow, I got to think deeper how can I contact with my dad if my dad is still alive somewhere out there. Who knows, one day am able to be the first whom contact with my dad and all the missing passengers. All I need is to remove 'I'''M'.

Copyright by Nai Boon Mee Sararaks (2017)

Time pass so fast, from day to months and am on my way to my first lecturer class. While am waiting for class start, I had some chat with my new college friends. Her name is Molly. She is very cute girl and was also interesting in astronomy. So, we got each other as best buddy in our education and research. She told me, before she came to this university, she was sad.

"It is just a cat, don't be sad." Her cat lose a day before she need to leave her home for education here.

"Am not Sad, Hurmey. Am focusing all my love to kitty." Kitty was her pet name.

"Then you found back her?"

Copyright by Nai Boon Mee Sararaks (2017)

"Of course. I found back Kitty, just few house after my house, Kitty was at my neighborhood house playing with another cats."

"Wow! How you knew Kitty is at that house?"

"First I never knew anything about Kitty lose, but after few seconds in silent, thinking what I need to do, in sudden I think about her heart beat. I always knew my Kitty heart beat was super faster than mine, so I close my eyes and keep focus on her heart beating in my mind, to kept me focus, I need to make my self empty, as empty as nothing can pop in my mind in sudden. So, in just a few seconds, a thought came to me in a visual, Kitty is at few house nearby with some other cats."

Copyright by Nai Boon Mee Sararaks (2017)

"Wonderful!"

Since then, I found her. I told my dad to take care of Kitty well, and we put Kitty back to the cage."

"Poor Kitty, she is no longer freedom then after you found her missing."

"What can I do, it all about not losing her again. My dad won't find Kitty, my mom also busy all day long. Who will? Am here in university."

"You will pretty missed Kitty then."

"Sure I will. Will back once every two weeks and hug Kitty then. You too can come along for a weekend holiday in my house."

Copyright by Nai Boon Mee Sararaks (2017)

"Sure, I will."

"Come, is time for our class. Let's walk in."

"Let's go. I hope it will be a very interesting class of our day today."

"Sure will, it's all about the journey to the stars up in the sky. We are the astronomers."

I was excited to know more about the class, and who is my perfect lecturer of the semester. I in sudden knew one point that if heart beat is they key in knowing a lose live cat, can it applied into human beings? Can it be the key to know where is my dad? But how can I know my dad heart beat? I've never heard before then. I guess I need to tell this great news to my mom as soon I arrive home

Copyright by Nai Boon Mee Sararaks (2017)

for my weekend break. As far as I concern, heart beat in our body never stop pumping for the entire life since the day we were in our mom journey to see the world. If this is possible, can the secret juice create by my dad can be the only gear up for the heart beat in connecting the unknown energy somewhere in our earth to make a contact with my dad, and if can it would be great every single peoples whom missed their missing love one can do the same thing.

But in my matter popped in my mind, how possible one person thoughts can be the same with the others. If my dads's juice is the formula in getting a contact with them, then what's next? Can it be all the missing passengers' families did the same thing and reply the same thoughts in visual that the answer to know the location is somewhere created with the unknown visual through our neurosis inside our mind. If the thoughts of all are the same visual, I pretty sure that connecting them is possible, it is just no one and not even one teacher, kick starter doing and not even one will do the same, beside this would be the craziest act of mankind again, which mankind could not believe that the imposible is actualy a possible matter, is what mass that created all masses all over the world in getting our mind calm down for not thinking deeper inside our mind. This is also the same incident happened to our world, my time where the 'Mind Syndrome' blasted the entire world as one of the hot news in all front page,

Copyright by Nai Boon Mee Sararaks (2017)

medias, and newspapers. No one is going to do, because everyone are fear in getting the truth out there, but if no one is going to do, who will then? But when one person start doing and the result is radically impossible to possible, the next and next and next till round over the world overnight hero's and heroin's, came from no where in sudden took over the city as the leader of city, land, and which ever place they born. Just imagine, one person can save the 60% of educational student, and graduates from this unknown 'Mind Syndrome' but one thing that the leaders ask to cure the patient is, no journalist and low ranking doctors is allow to enter the intensive care unit room without any authorized, and only the allowed doctors are the higher management, and board of the directors are

Copyright by Nai Boon Mee Sararaks (2017)

allowed to view the touch on the patient heal the entire syndrome.

From what I know, that was the touch of love from the healers. The healers are the person kind of spirituality, that are able to connect one dimensional stage of life with another realms of life out from body, the astral. Even in that history of mankind, the country leader that time are panic and do not know what to do next, the touch of the country leader that time are touchless. After over night, many turn up from all over the place in the countries in getting the patient healed. Since then, the ruling system change, only for those whom can heal the world syndrome mass is our true leader of

Copyright by Nai Boon Mee Sararaks (2017)

the land, since then the citizens declare the land of love all over the major cities in the world.

In my mind now, am I the first to be the kick start like the one step forward in healing the patient? Am I capable enough to contact with the missing one?

I am weird in this content popped in my mind, if we missed someone we can feel them the existing, but can't we have a clear visual of them somewhere like the cats story?

Next, if let say our late deceased grandmother. We knew that she is no longer in this world timeline, we are the witness of the death, the cremation of death ceremony and we knew she is not in this world, from time to time we can had a

Copyright by Nai Boon Mee Sararaks (2017)

dream that she is at some beautiful place somewhere not belongs to earth. We can see that beauty, we can flew and talk to them in a cave light up with white candle, aren't this as a dream or a messenger from our late grandmother telling us not to worry about her, she is already placed in a beautiful place not belongs to earth. Somewhere out there, a heaven possible or a home where some of us believe that when we die, we will go back to the home where we beginning came from to earth for birth.

In my dad's incident, I do not have a visual that my dad is confirm declared death, because there is no debris found years after years.

Copyright by Nai Boon Mee Sararaks (2017)

My friend, Molly said life is like a Wi-Fi at any restaurants, or Wi-Fi hotspot place. When we can connect with them, we need a password. When we have the password we are only able to connect to the Wi-Fi server. After connected, only we are able to Google the world out there for so many information, some information are false and some are true, even some are created like this novel for the purpose of love and understanding that some facts happens in our life must be a reason for, and nothings happen for no reason. Having a wifi connection lose, we need to recover the password. If we unable to connect, we still can see the name of the Wi-Fi appear through the air and pop out in our mobile, and laptops. So, in my case, if my dad is not connected with me, my mom

Copyright by Nai Boon Mee Sararaks (2017)

sure able to connect with him because the connection server is still there but the matter is without the password to view the where is the location, in getting this view clear, we need a password.

Am sure now, the password is the heart beats, and the electricity in getting this works is my dad's juice. That's far for now am thinking while walking to the lecturer hall. Searching for the place to seat with my best buddy Molly.

"Molly, let's sit right in front here, ok?"

"Sure, it was close to understand more and we can ask question easily later on."

"Wonderful."

Copyright by Nai Boon Mee Sararaks (2017)

CHAPTER 6

"UNIVERSE , youniverse

begin with you, yourself." Said Professor Dr. Wazt Benson. He is one of the famous symbiosis professor in and have a deep research about astronomy, and extraterrestrial research for space, time and relativity.

Professor kept silent, look around and stop his eye to one of the student. The student is Hurmey Maruka. He look into her shirt, with a sign of 'I love my dad'. He then kept silent for one second continue his lecture.

Copyright by Nai Boon Mee Sararaks (2017)

"If mankind truly search deeper into the bottom of the heart, we can always feel our love one is always there, the heart beats are always connected as one melody, the heart positioning system (HPS) is our ancient communication radar, is not a joke but it is always in my mind since when I am childhood journey, this knowledge was not guide from school, not anywhere but it is natural came in me. Today I share with all of you, we human body and mind are very complex and unbelievable sometime we never knew unexpected things can happen anytime in the terms of elements of life. We are easy to absorbs something new in the society and through the media community, but we hardly absorbs things which are already hidden for years in our life and deep in the core of our

Copyright by Nai Boon Mee Sararaks (2017)

mind." Professor then wrote some word on the white board.

He wrote few sentence.

'Looking peoples around you, there is an answer hidden in the micro terms and condition.'

I took my breath in and stay focus. I look into my shirt, and I miss my dad while listening to this awesome lecturer. Listening to his lecture and pen down each and every voices came in my ears which is I knew it is an important for me to note down on my notebook.

Yourself is the strength of all creation. All of you here in this lecturer hall are up coming to be the future leaders, and you going to lead humanity

Copyright by Nai Boon Mee Sararaks (2017)

to the next dimensional stage of consciousness level. We all improved each other, but not to harm each other, this is what human are. If we harm each other, our world must have some gaps somewhere that separates us as human, and theirs as human with multi venture dark heart. No one are allow to create the fear among us here. See around you here, turn to the left and right of this lecturer hall, see among yourself, what shirt all of you wear right now? Each of you here carry the energy in you, carry the particles of messenger to life, to your friends nearby you right now!"… Professor write on the board, 'The Future is now'.

…But not all of us are aware off the happening nearby. Just turn around, what are the

Copyright by Nai Boon Mee Sararaks (2017)

messenger brought by your friend now, he or she represent the energy state level in their consciousness life. In the terms of symbiosis, male and female? Does it be as simple as sperm and ovum? Not really. the atom of the stars reach earth and they are symbiotic with the nature on earth which is the elements we knew like fire, soil, diamonds, gold, water, air, mass and more. These atom then enter the sole energy of a male and sperms are ejaculated in the female virginal for the earthily symbiosis to begin take place in the womb of the mother to take a human birth process and perform good of the human purpose and depart the soul leaving the body back on earth in it's environment again and again. Look around."

Copyright by Nai Boon Mee Sararaks (2017)

Professor kept silent and students start to pay attention on each other.

Hurmey Maruka turn to her right, see the shirt of Molly, her friend. Printed on the shirt, was positive words "Never give up! I am waiting for you." Hurmey, was so amaze with the lecturer talk and in a sudden she was touched by the heart.

Molly turn to the left, and she saw a small picture of hello kitty cat printed on Hurmeys' shirt. Her mind flash back to her home, thinking back her lovely Kitty in the cage, what is Kitty doing now?

Lecturer continue his speech,

Copyright by Nai Boon Mee Sararaks (2017)

"Have you all aware right now, the beginning of our class today, all of us are getting closer by what we suppose to do in our life. If am not about to ask all of you here turn and look each other, channeling your frequencies into an answer, won't you aware off the language I am trying to tell you now? This is the language of the universe, in you and you and all of you here. Without this languages, I believe none of you here would understand deeper into the ocean of the universe up there, down here or at the cosmic level of the stars, the planets and the star system here for our earth and more out there uncountable. To understand deeper about what is happening out there no matter in the topics of astronomers, or your own personal matters, everything start inside

Copyright by Nai Boon Mee Sararaks (2017)

here, right inside yourself. Is you, when you start to explore and understand yourself, you soon and sooner will understand the world, and when the world understand you, you will have the opportunity to go further and understand the universe up there, when the universe understand you, you will have a further more journey to understand more unknown planets, and galaxies, and star systems out there… professor drink some water

…the most weird common behavior of mankind here on earth is, peoples tends not to understand themselves even some practitioner doctors today, but they are able to understand

Copyright by Nai Boon Mee Sararaks (2017)

peoples, understand patients out there. How can this possible, now you ask me? Any question?"

Hurmey raise hand up.

"Yes, my little star. Where you from and what you want to ask me? I have 7 seconds just for you begin now."

"I am from the seven hills of love, does the 'Mind Syndrome' face by most students years back right over here and around the world is begin with not understand themselves?, Thank you."

"You may remain seated. Thank you for you diamond stars question."

Lecturer walk to the board, he write a sentence.

Copyright by Nai Boon Mee Sararaks (2017)

'Mind is mass, and mass is energy.'

"All of you, read this out loud."

Everyone followed and read out loud.

"Mind is mass, and mass is energy." Students was so amaze with his talk.

Now, let me tell you the true story what's happening in our history and our past. Mankind are very soft, we are like a sponge, we absorbed anything in a seconds. But we do not know what we absorbed can hurt, harm, change the entire circle of our life, or for the good benefit of our future and all peoples around the earth. Mankind thinks that they are pretty smart with what they have right now in 'their time' but in fact wrong.

Copyright by Nai Boon Mee Sararaks (2017)

What they have in their time, makes them 'just feel' save, and smart but those things they have in their time soon make them even worst. They are lazy to think, lazy to act, lazy to do their work, and even worst they are lazy to go toilet. Am sorry, If am wrong. Correct me if am wrong again, in their time, they even go to toilet using their technology gadget device. If you can log in, click on the screen I go in the toilet today and depart, it means you're done going to the toilet. You see, there is a world of timeline happening in that time of now, and 'their time' which is not our actual timeline. In our time we knew some of the impossible are always possible for all of us. Why? Because we knew our human potential limits can go beyond the imagination.

Copyright by Nai Boon Mee Sararaks (2017)

"Albert Einstein did said in centuries during his time, he said…

"Imagination is more important than knowledge, knowledge is limited, imagination encircle the world. Added, Education is not the training of fact, but the training of the mind to think." Albert Einstein.

…this is why, when our students in our time believe that knowledge and the books provided by makes them smart, but their body could not accept the knowledge given by themselves. Due to this matter, their brains stopped functioning and everything turns down. Is the same guys and girls here, if you would just fall in love with someone you love you will always in love, but of you would

Copyright by Nai Boon Mee Sararaks (2017)

just having a relationship with some one due to his or her attraction and desire of sex, if would rather fall apart in distance one day near future. This same goes to our brain, when we are educated since our childhood playing all electronics gadgets, we are not aware of the future that a little part of history can destroy the entire brain system works. Am here in this class not suppose to give you eat what you suppose to not to eat now, but when it's the perfect time for you to have your first breakfast of your mind today for your first semester here in our University of Lovdom, then be my pleasure to treat all of you here, today. With this, I end my class and welcoming all of you to this university, may this journey brings you the next level of understanding of love and wisdom that matters all

Copyright by Nai Boon Mee Sararaks (2017)

education and humanity improve. If you all have any question, please do so by email me anytime possible. With love and respect, and with love and wisdom, I again end my class for today. Have a great day ahead. Professor take his belonging and books, and walk off the class smartly with his pink Nike shoes. Maybe it was the favorite colors of his choices. Students stand up and thanks with bow, and touch their heart with their right hand palms. Everyone feel so honor in having their first mind breakfast in understanding the beginning of the new education here was a perfect journey. They all the present students will never ever make mistake again from what had happened in the past years students fall apart with their life just to understand that smart is the way of mind.

Copyright by Nai Boon Mee Sararaks (2017)

I saw many students carries their personal languages in their energy level representing the languages of the universe, some are far walking down the hall that truly match me. I saw, 'Are you thinking of me'. Again, I saw 'Nothing is false and nothing is true, is all about you.'

I walk down few steps because am just sitting right front of the hall, and in sudden I saw a language saying,

'We are all waiting for you.'

'Journey back home, through time.'

This languages makes my fur stood up and in sudden my mind was getting deeper inside, what

Copyright by Nai Boon Mee Sararaks (2017)

is all about this languages of unknown universe group in a hall of my first mind breakfast.

I kept quite and continue my life in university until waiting for the two weeks after, I can return home for my break and that is the time I will break my mom Wi-Fi for the password. Before that, I will find the password for my mom.

Copyright by Nai Boon Mee Sararaks (2017)

CHAPTER 7

"Mom! Am back. Mom! Where are you mom?". Hurmey searching for her mom. Starting from her own home office, to her room.

She knock the room door.

"Mom! You in?"

The door was unlocked. Normally her mom door was locked all time. Sudden Hurmey had a bad feeling.

Hurmey open the door and look around in the room where her mom sleep.

Copyright by Nai Boon Mee Sararaks (2017)

"Hello, anybody? Mom? Where're you mom."

Hurmey walk out the room. Walk down the stair case and look around in the fruits kitchen. The kitchen was maze up with avocado, red apple, and lemon. Leave over dad's mystery juice in the fruits blender. One mug of lemon, mixed red apple and avocado juice leave with a note of letter place beside. She picked up the letter and read.

Copyright by Nai Boon Mee Sararaks (2017)

Dear my little lovely daughter,

Hurmey Maruka, mom missed you a lot. Do you missed mom here?

Mom knew you are about to arrived home today morning, but mom cannot wait you anymore. Mom need to go up the nearby seven hill tower junction and meet up with moms spirituals' friends house. Remember the lady that mom always told you, lady with the name Judith. She and all mom

Copyright by Nai Boon Mee Sararaks (2017)

friends are waiting for today good news. Mom prepared one mug of dads' secret juice here for just for you. It is an important day for us to meet up overnight camp and I hope once you read this letter, do drink this and come right forward over the junction of seven hill, Judith house. We all already drink your dad secrets' juice over here. All of us are waiting for you, did mom told you that you're special? We are all waiting for what you've been ready

Copyright by Nai Boon Mee Sararaks (2017)

for so long. Heart to heart, love to love, mind to mind, and vibration to vibration, the secret juice that dad create for us are well respect in everyone hearts in the future. Maybe, it is dads' time capsule kept by him for the entire future world peoples. Not to forget, bring some extra blankets and sneaks for mom and yours too. If any leave over fresh apples, and oranges in the kitchen, Himalaya pink salt and strawberries, please bring over here.

Copyright by Nai Boon Mee Sararaks (2017)

Mom wait for you, love you always. Let's make the earth history proud again. Let's make the timeline of our earth history come back to life.

Love Mom,

07 March Love

Copyright by Nai Boon Mee Sararaks (2017)

Hurmey pick up the mug and drink her dads' secret juice. In sudden, she saw another letter at the corner of the kitchen, she put down the mug and pick up the letter. She read at the end signature. Is her friend Judith wrote to her.

Copyright by Nai Boon Mee Sararaks (2017)

Dear Stacey Hurmey,

I think is about time we need to help you out on your concern with your beloved missing husband. Your lovely savior daughter are well ready enough on her way back to home, you got to come to our juice bar meet up gathering next morning. Be early before the sun rise in the 8th March, and we will help you out on your daughters mission in contacting your beloved husband. Remember before the sun

Copyright by Nai Boon Mee Sararaks (2017)

rise, make sure you get ready with all the juice you prepared. Be early wake up, and arrived before the sun rise.

With love,

Judith, and the spiritual juice team.

Copyright by Nai Boon Mee Sararaks (2017)

Hurmey quickly packed my belongings and blanket for her mom and herself. It was cold up there. It is close to the six hill. The hill they stay was the seven hill from the bottom. She need to walk up to the junction of seven hill later. She was so excited and she mark the calendar in a circle, seven and eight. On the eight, 'she write welcome back home, love you dad.'

This was the journey she waiting for so long. While she packed her belonging. Hurmey then bring the outdoor hill booster Wi-Fi device, so that she can share her discoveries to the world hours before the welcoming back moment.

The world peoples yet know what is all about they are doing, they are about to keep this

Copyright by Nai Boon Mee Sararaks (2017)

secret till the final moment and share to the world when the perfect time come, she close all doors and back doors. She pack all her items, wear her shoes and close the door. She walk few steps out from her house. Look at the right, someone is there for her. Someone come to her house waiting just in front of her house, seating at the garden bench. Guess who?

"Hurmey!"

"Robert! What are you doing here in the morning? Aren't you suppose to open your grocer later?"

"My workers are taking care for 24 hours from now."

Copyright by Nai Boon Mee Sararaks (2017)

"Wonderful, how you knew my house here? You make me surprise."

"Thank you, is your mom. Your mom came to my Fruits Rainbow when you were at university."

"My Mom?"

"Ya, your mom told me all about you. About your unknown discovery journey."

"How can my mom knows that?"

"Maybe your mom has her own secret too, haha…" "Her spiritual friends maybe."

"Ya, maybe you're correct. They are so close to the nature, I believe they know what they

Copyright by Nai Boon Mee Sararaks (2017)

are suppose to know now, and you too you know what you going to do next, am I correct?"

Yes, am ready for all this moment am waiting for.

"So, is my mom plan telling you to wait me and accompany me up to hill."

"Yes, you mom was a very lovely women. I wish she can meet up with her husband in 24 hours later."

"Wonderful. I hope too, I am ready to contact dad again. I wish I can hug my dad for the first time."

"Come, let me help you carry few heavy items up for you. The small part you can carry by yourself."

Copyright by Nai Boon Mee Sararaks (2017)

"Lovely you. Thanks."

"They then carry things up, walk up slowly to the hill. The junction of the seven hill."

"Welcome, it's my happiness and love to share this moment with you. How's life at university for the first two weeks?"

"Wonderful, I learn lots of thing. In fact in just two weeks, I knew few add value on my research."

Both of them was so happy sharing their lovely moment up to the hill. When she arrive at the hill, they put their things up. Hurmey Maruka hug her mom right away,

"Mom, miss you so much."

Copyright by Nai Boon Mee Sararaks (2017)

"I miss you too. I am so worry about you, worry you couldn't go further in your mind keep thinking about dad."

"Am fine. Am good mom."

"On the other hand, mom too worry your first two weeks education over there could hunted you there. It was the best university in the city of love."

"Thanks for you care mom."

"Have you drink the secret juice mom prepared for you?"

"Yes, yes. I drink all of it."

Copyright by Nai Boon Mee Sararaks (2017)

"Great, come lets begin some work over here. They are waiting for us over the hill corner, especially for you."

"Really?, Oh ya Mom, introduce you to my friend, Robert."

"Yeah, Mom's knows him well. He is your dads' to his dad best buddy during the old time."

"Mom, you knew it earlier, why don't you tell me while we are on call."

"Mom knew you're busy at university. Yes, aren't mom told you before that you are special? Special means we don't have to communicate through a phone, we use heart to heart. Ok, come

Copyright by Nai Boon Mee Sararaks (2017)

lets go, they're just the corner of the communication tower waiting for us…

…Lovely memory. So, mom welcome you and introduce you to our expert in welcoming back our missing flight for years, Mr.Robert. Is all your time now, Robert."

"Is my pleasure." Robert smile to Hurmey mom and feeling exited to use his dads' leave over knowledge in helping Hurmey.

"Thank you, lots to learn from you soon." Hurmey smile.

"If everything goes smooth for the next 24 hours from now, you can start share our plan to the world. Their time and our time is totally different.

Copyright by Nai Boon Mee Sararaks (2017)

It is almost one day faster than the actual missing day and time." Robert replied.

Hurmey excited what's going to happen next,

"Mom, since when mom become so energetic in knowing all about dad and such a great researcher?"

"Mom is always a great fruits researcher. Remember, is your dad and is my lovely husband coming back. Is all about life out there, so many peoples and families members are waiting for our good news from here."

While talking, Hurmey search for a power socket and plug in her Wi-Fi and set the Wi-Fi setting signal into 15 numerical in order.

Copyright by Nai Boon Mee Sararaks (2017)

Robert walk close to Hurmey, he look around the sky. It was a dark clear sky, with so many stars.

"Hurmey, make sure the signal of your Wi-Fi hotspot is strong enough for all of us here boosting up to the other part of time."

"Sure, sure, I will ensure the signal and the power supply is enough. Anyway, what's the 15 digits of hotspot name we will use? I am setting up now."

"Hurmey, set for me 1,3,1,4,9,9,1,1,1,2,1,5,2,2,5 into the hotspot setting."

Copyright by Nai Boon Mee Sararaks (2017)

"Sure, I will. Hurmey key in 131499111215225.

Took her breath in and out

"Done."

"Great job Hurmey." Robert look on his cellphone display connectivity and appear the signal setting up by Hurmey.

It was very windy at the top of the hill. Robert and his spiritual team are preparing to boots up the signal to the other part of time using their intelligence by sitting down into a formation of two rows which is connected to Mr.Robert in the front. 7 peoples in the left, 7 peoples in the right, one in front was Mr.Robert, and another one at the

Copyright by Nai Boon Mee Sararaks (2017)

back was a she, Ms.Venesia. Both Ms.Venesia and Mr.Robert are the universe player which able to contact one layer of our earth to the another layer of time whenever needed in timeline. Both of them knew that our present time is already mass up with cold air mass, and there is no meaning of time constancy future, past and now. We are actually living in the time of our own mind.

16 peoples get well ready sitting in the position ordered by Mr.Robert and Venesia. They touch each other back, and start to transmit out the numerical set by Mr.Robert to them in visualize and transmit out to the universe as a genuine signal. They do not know the possibility of receiving, but they knew it will happen.

Copyright by Nai Boon Mee Sararaks (2017)

The diagram of their position as below:

Ms.Venesia

+

Male + Female

Male + Female

Male + Female

Male + Female

Male + Female

Male + Female

Male + Female

-

Mr.Robert

Copyright by Nai Boon Mee Sararaks (2017)

This is the imagination of an author connecting one time to another time in sending out a signal to different part of our world without using any high technology, but just our own mind transmitted out in visual.

Hurmey was not involved, she is sitting in the corner to ensure the signal is well visible.

Robert, is about the time now, let us all begin focus and slowly transmitted out to the air space and let's all welcoming our lost plan through time.

Copyright by Nai Boon Mee Sararaks (2017)

CHAPTER 8

"Lumpur control Malaysian, Three Seven Zero." MH370

ATC "Malaysian Three Seven Zero radar good morning climb flight level two five zero.

Morning level two five zero, Malaysian Three Seven Zero" MH370

ATC "Malaysian Three Seven Zero climb flight level three five zero." ATC

Flight level three five zero Malaysian Three Seven Zero…MH370

Copyright by Nai Boon Mee Sararaks (2017)

Malaysian Three Seven Zero Maintaining level three five zero. MH370

ATC "Malaysian Three Seven Zero…

Malaysian Three Seven Zero maintaining level three five zero, MH370

ATC "Malaysian Three Seven Zero"

ATC "Malaysian Three Seven Zero contact Ho Chi Minh 120 decimal 9 Good night."

"Good night Malaysian Three Seven Zero." MH370.

Kuala Lumpur Radar, conversations between ATC and Flight 370 from pre-departure to

Copyright by Nai Boon Mee Sararaks (2017)

final contact (00:25 AM – 01:19 AM), Feb 8 year 2014.

"Robert and all, is the time now. Let us transmit out the code up to the air space and open up the portal of time counting from 10-0." Venesia begin to give order.

10,9,8,7,6,5,4,3,2,1,0

All start to stay focus and visualized repeatedly 1314991112152225, 1314991112152225, 1314991112152225, 1314991112152225, 1314991112152225, 1314991112152225, 1314991112152225, 1314991112152225,

Copyright by Nai Boon Mee Sararaks (2017)

8 times repeated to transmitted out these frequency back to the time where the final conversation took place in the year 2014, 8 March.

"Malaysian Three Seven Zero contact Ho Chi Minh." The Captain trying to contact the Ho Chi Minh air space but no one replied. The entire Boeing getting very cold inside.

"Captain, It getting a sudden cold in our flight, what's is happening?"

"Stay calm, I am trying to contact Ho Chi Minh air space but yet no respond."

"Malaysian Three Seven Zero contact Ho Chi Minh." Repeated again from MH370 flight communication.

Copyright by Nai Boon Mee Sararaks (2017)

"The transponder is turn off automatically. What we should do next?"

"Look in front, we are not in the air space anymore. What was that tunnel heading us to?

"Captain, turn to the left direction, we are still far behind to turn back to the nearest air port."

The captain took his decision, to turn back to the nearby Penang International Airport but fail in sudden. The energy of the tunnel pulling in the entire Boeing 777 forward in a very fast speed. The passengers do not know anything while everyone are sleeping. The passenger seats are well not interrupted with any noise. Only the front Captain can see and feel what is happening in the front.

Copyright by Nai Boon Mee Sararaks (2017)

"It's getting very cold out there. Inside too."

"There's no thunder, and no rain, but it was an unknown space we're entering here."

The Captain is still under control.

"I will hold my direction and try our best to stay calm."

No respond. In sudden a replied from an unknown signal. Beeping and again beeping, the entire flight was in the heavy vibration mode. Passengers start to woke up and the air stewardess and steward calm the passengers down informing it was the cloud that make the chair and the entire flight vibrate repeatedly like a signal code.

Copyright by Nai Boon Mee Sararaks (2017)

In sudden all mobile screen turn on automatically, the screen of the Boeing 777 auto display Ω131499111215225 Ω

The pilot respond the replied

"This is Malaysian Three Seven Zero heading from Kuala Lumpur International Airport to Beijing."

"Malaysia Three Seven Zero…

"Malaysia Three Seven Zero…

This is the rescue team from the galactic control tower. We are now heading your time to the future.

"Malaysian Three Seven Zero, what does it mean? Who is in charge over this Boeing? We are

Copyright by Nai Boon Mee Sararaks (2017)

sending out our ping signal out to our air space now."

"Galactic control tower, you're now heading forward in three hundred and seventy years from your time. The air space position you in now is too high and it's getting cold very fast."

"Malaysian Three Seven Zero, what should we do next."

"Don't worry, we are channeling your space time to the perfect time in near future for an emergency landing at the nearest international Airport."

Copyright by Nai Boon Mee Sararaks (2017)

What is all about, Captain? How can it be? The date, time and direction are in mass now. The control screen in in an auto locked.

The pilot radar screen coordinate appear

Ω1314991112152225Ω for an emergency landing to the nearest future timeline.

Let's wait and see what's happening next. That tunnel are so frightening. We can felt any shaky at all, but it just when deep into the direction without any sky, clouds and horizon.

All passengers watch, display time sudden stop at 10:10PM in the evening. Passengers calm themselves down and do not know what is happening until they were given order by the crew.

Copyright by Nai Boon Mee Sararaks (2017)

In a sudden, the entire air space that the flight heading to disappear and they entered into an unknown space which is in pink horizon down to the earth. All communication sudden back to normal. The captain quickly remote his flight and trying to communicate nearby landing exit.

"Malaysian Three Seven Zero, we are now entering unknown air space, permission for an emergency landing."

"Penang International Airport Communication Tower, this is officer Paul speaking. Malaysian Three Seven Zero, your are allowed now for an emergency landing."

"Malaysian Three Seven Zero, copy that. We are now route to an emergency landing."

Copyright by Nai Boon Mee Sararaks (2017)

Captain, and the entire crew do not know what is all happening.

The airport was crowed by so many peoples around the world waiting for their return. The city was never the same from the time they depart. Much more advance. The flight Boeing 777 MH370 take the final landing on the Penang International Airport, that was the route they heading to during on the unknown space.

Police office and ambulance waiting for their arrival at the front door ladders, health officer from all over the countries did wait for them. Families and friends from far behind the glass view. The entire airport was crowed. That was the only day the entire world air space stop the entire

Copyright by Nai Boon Mee Sararaks (2017)

flight operation at air space just for waiting the flight MH370 safely landing at the nearby airport. When they open up the door, the first step out was the captain. He view the entire environment of the air port, it was never be the same again. The tower was control by a core of strong magnetic tower at the corner of the airport which he did not ever see before. He look around were these peoples are familiar with him? The Prime Minister stand at the main entrance with red carpet welcome back the Captain for his return.

Somehow the story never end that happy. Although they make their return, the paramedic and health team direct all crew and passengers on board to another road where a bus waiting for them.

Copyright by Nai Boon Mee Sararaks (2017)

All the passengers were admitted into quarantine, medical office ask so many question about what's happening up there but not even a single answer were answer by the passengers, and the crew. No one answered, all in silent.

"I've arrived safely, and now this is the question you dump to me? Was this question important or the life of the passengers are much more important? I've bring back all safe, and what I receive was a quarantine and cannot meet with my family members?"

After 30 day later. The government do not have any choice and to release all passengers back home meeting up with their family. The case of this missing flight that hidden for so many years

Copyright by Nai Boon Mee Sararaks (2017)

since the 8 March 2014, was listed as unknown incident whereby there is no answer from crew and passengers on board.

Copyright by Nai Boon Mee Sararaks (2017)

CHAPTER 9

Day never grown old, time never shift back,

the seconds I stood out from this house. It was the day I come back. But, everything change. I cannot differentiate what is old and what is new. My wife are still the same, my daughter are still the same, never grow old same as me but one thing is the years and the time change. I cannot deny of this unpredictable earth given to me. Things that happen to each and everyone of us there must be a reason for. Nothing happens for no reason.

Copyright by Nai Boon Mee Sararaks (2017)

"Dad, finally you're back. You know what, we've been waited you for so long, with an additional of 30 days quarantine. It was our pain that you heal us today, dad. I love you."

"Hurmey, my lovely daughter. Dad love you too. Nothing happen for no reason. What dad believe from you, you're special. Because of you, we are here unite again." Hugging each other.

"Miss you dad."

"Where's my lovely wife?"

Hurmey mom from kitchen walk out with the secret juice and a welcome cake for his lovely husband. Walk so fast and hug together with her daughter, and lovely husband. The kiss each other.

Copyright by Nai Boon Mee Sararaks (2017)

"You know, you make all of us worry about you for years we can't even sleep, watch any news, because we knew all the news out there was a lie."

"Heart to heart, dad." Replied Hurmey.

This was a journey that Hurmey Maruka experienced in her life, but things that even more weird is her dad. He did not even know what is happening, and how can the time consume be so complicated in our lovely earth.

No matter how it goes, they are back together as one happy family, the government then close the case. Peoples start to forget and ignore what is happening, as long as they've come back to their love one.

Copyright by Nai Boon Mee Sararaks (2017)

Life is like a projection on a screen at the final destiny, if you feel that you want to watch again, you may repeat and watch like a memories. But some peoples out there do not have the memories kept by them even in a single phone video recording, or a photos. What can you do with only memories in your mind? Visualize the moments together without knowing the time, years, and seconds, the love one you recall are alive in our heart that connect to our mind. This connection are powerful enough to know where we are heading to without acknowledge any highly potential technology of mankind created, and how can we know that life on earth is just a timeline of an unknown data given to us from day by day, time through time without a single words that even

Copyright by Nai Boon Mee Sararaks (2017)

we tried to understand, try to search for it, but it will remain as a clue. The further we go, the more we compile our data, the higher possibility of speculation able to convert as the missing puzzle. When the puzzle are fixed, we will see the beauty of our lost visual that we always waiting for, our love one.

-The End-

Copyright by Nai Boon Mee Sararaks (2017)

"This novel of science fiction novel written by me, as an author was from my owned imaginary base mind to public reading.

It was my job to give the happy ending story which is different than other writers wrote in the past. Not even one written down are real, and do not relates with any truth. It was only a fictional journey. I know my written words are not so well in words, but I admit I love to improve my writing skills near future.

Copyright by Nai Boon Mee Sararaks (2017)

Personally I am proud to write this to the world, as one of the healing of mind. Personally I would like to take this opportunity to sent out my love and concern to all missing passengers families out there and if any translator would love to re-write in other language, please do so helping me hand to hand and share to the world."

With love to the entire world, let us share and hug our moments together and believe in faith, we shall near to every corner of an answer that hidden in the micro circle.

Copyright by Nai Boon Mee Sararaks (2017)

www.ingramcontent.com/pod-product-compliance
Lightning Source LLC
Chambersburg PA
CBHW031314160726

47993CB00001B/409